Kealy Connor Lonning

Our Amazing Blankets

Illustrator Lora Look

1

2

We're twins—a boy and girl,
and how we like to play!
Together, always—yes,
with lots of fun each day.

3

4

A blanket, we each have—
one's pink and one is blue.
Our blankets have been ours,
since we were born and new!

5

Amazing blankets—wow!
They share our many days.
Our blankets can be used
in oh, so many ways!

6

7

Our blankets help our pains,
and dry up all our tears.

9

They make us feel so safe,
and take away our fears.

10

Our blankets can be skirts,
we spin around and twirl.

12

13

14

Then hero capes we wear—
for super boy and girl.

15

Our wishes do come true.
We wish to reach the sky.
Our blankets are the best!
Our magic carpets fly!

17

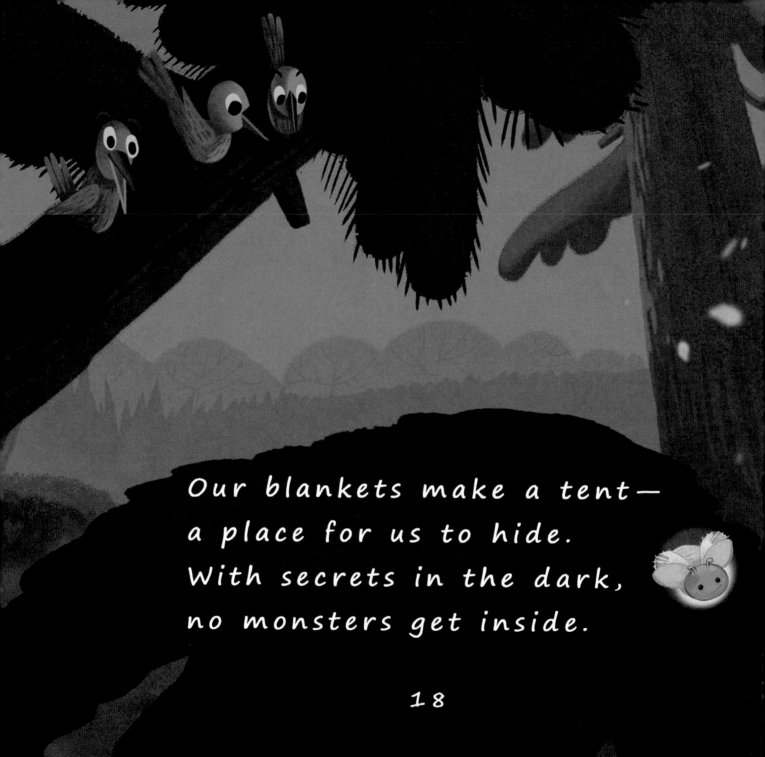

Our blankets make a tent—
a place for us to hide.
With secrets in the dark,
no monsters get inside.

18

They're with us everywhere.
Our blankets go outside.
They join us on the swings,

20

21

and also for a ride.

22

23

The two of us explore—
and through the woods we go.
Our blankets make us brave.
The bears are there, we know!

24

25

Our blankets feel so nice.
They line the treasure box,
that always gently holds,
our lovely leaves and rocks.

27

We like our picnics here,
on blankets on the floor.

28

To make a curtained stage,
they're hung up by the door.

Our blankets help us be
a princess in a gown,
and prince in royal robe,
who likes to wear a crown.

31

32

Our blankets, yes, we love.
We love each other, too!
We're lucky that we've got,
such awesome things to do.

33

Our blankets cover us.
They help us sleep at night.
We feel so warm and loved,
in blankets, wrapped up tight.

34

Our blankets will wear out,
and though the threads will fray,
our special bond is strong—
forever twins we'll stay.

38

Dedication

For my boy--girl twins, GABLE and GARA,
who have always inspired me with their
amazing imaginations!! When they were little,
they loved to create costumes and stories,
using their blankets for dramatic play.
Gable and Gara have always been awesome actors,
and their whole world was a magical stage. 😃😃

Love you forever,
my sweet, delightful, talented twinsies!! 🤍🖤 Love, Mom

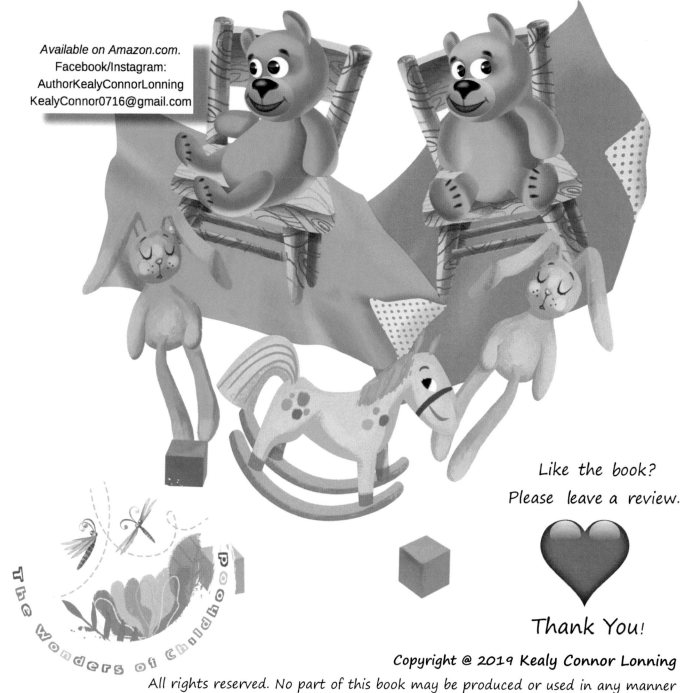

Like the book?
Please leave a review.

Thank You!

The Wonders of Childhood

Made in the USA
Monee, IL
24 March 2022